Sandy Creek
NEW YORK

An Imprint of Sterling Publishing
387 Park Avenue South
New York, NY 10016

Text © 2011 by Parragon Books Ltd
Illustrations © 2011 by Parragon Books Ltd

This 2013 edition published by Sandy Creek.

ISBN 978-1-4351-4727-0

Manufactured in Heshan, China
Lot #:
10 9 8 7 6 5 4 3 2 1

04/13

Say Please, Little Bear

Sandy Creek
NEW YORK

Daddy Bear and Little Bear were on the way to kindergarten.
But Little Bear kept wandering off.

"Keep hold of my hand, Little Bear!" said Daddy Bear.

"Go gently, Little Bear!" said Daddy Bear.

But Little Bear didn't listen.

"Little Bear, it isn't nice to grab!"

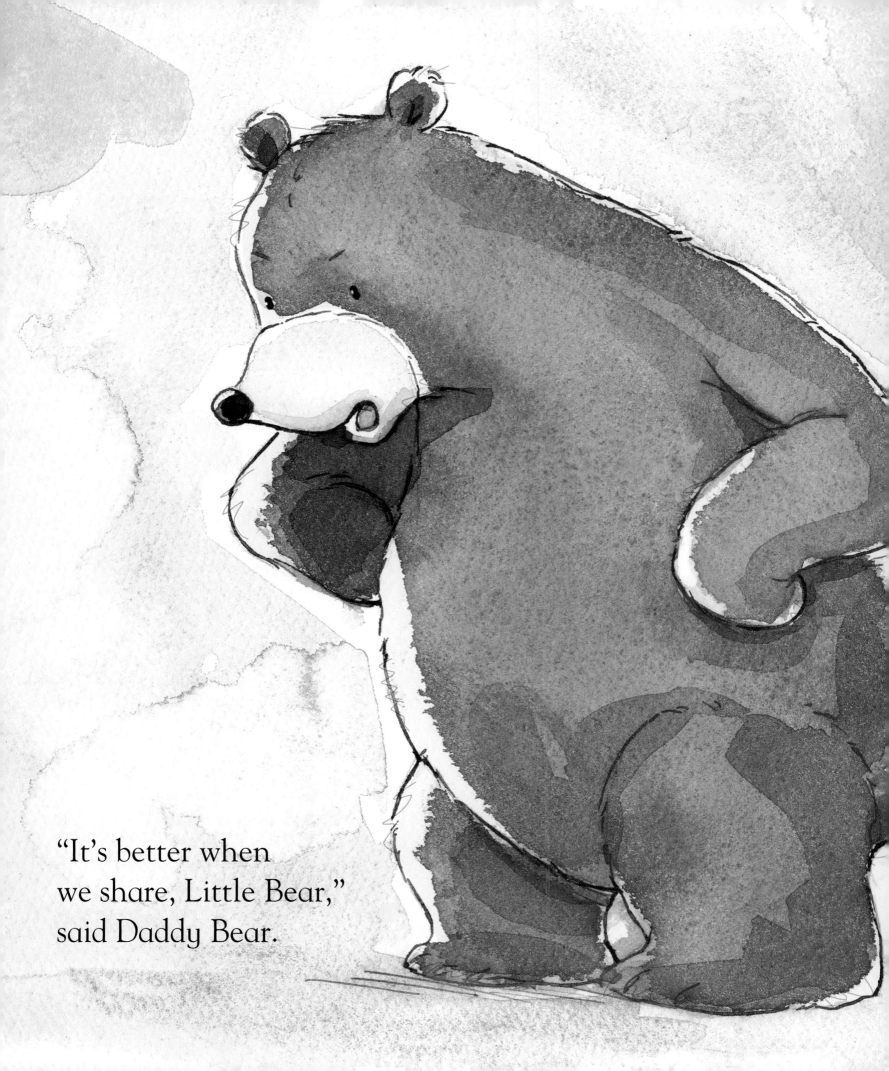

"It's better when
we share, Little Bear,"
said Daddy Bear.

Later, Daddy Bear took Little Bear to
Little Bunny's birthday party.
They went shopping on the way.
"Please hold my hand, Little Bear!"
said Daddy wearily.

Then something in the shop window
gave Daddy Bear an idea.
"Look, Little Bear," he said.
"That mouse wants
to speak to us!"

"Mouse wants to go to the party too, Little Bear," said Daddy Bear. "But he hates to be late!"

They got to Little Bunny's party on time.
Mouse whispered in Daddy Bear's ear.

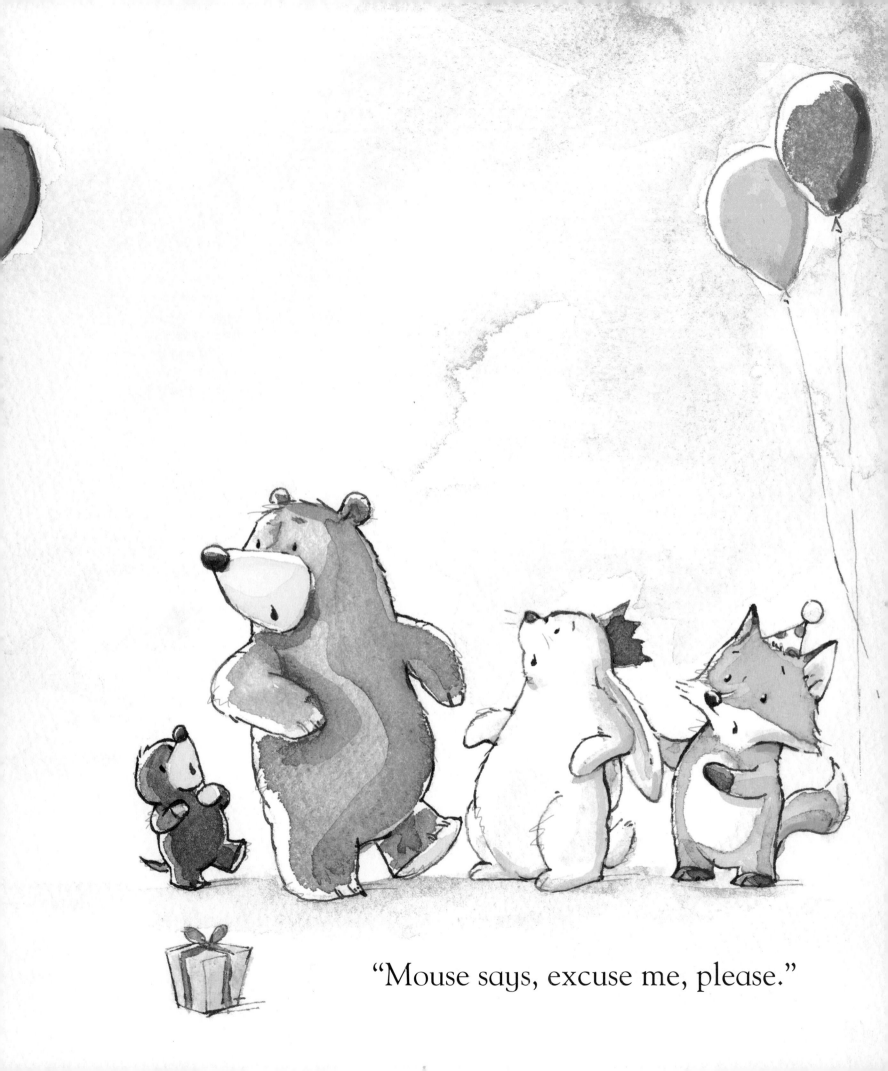

"Mouse says, excuse me, please."

Little Bear ran to play on the train.
Mouse whispered in Daddy Bear's ear.
"Mouse says,
can she have
a ride on the
train, please?"

Little Bear grabbed the popcorn from his friends.
Mouse whispered in Daddy Bear's ear.
"Mouse says, would *you* like some popcorn, Bunny
and Mole?"

When it was
time to go,
Little Bear
stood silently
on the doorstep.
"Mouse says,
thank you for
having me,"
said Daddy.

Little Bear looked at Mouse. Then he looked at Daddy Bear. Then he looked at Little Bunny's mom, and said, "And thank you for having me."

"Oh, thank you for coming,
Little Bear," smiled Little Bunny's mom.

"You and Mouse can come
and play anytime."

"Mouse likes the way
you said thank you,"
said Daddy Bear.

"And so do I."